W9-BYH-654

E   Allcroft, Britt.
ALL   Britt Allcroft's magic
           adventures of Mumfie

Copyright © Britt Allcroft (Mumfie) Limited 2001. All rights reserved under
International and Pan-American Copyright Conventions. Published in the United States by
Random House, Inc., New York, and simultaneously in Canada by Random House of Canada
Limited, Toronto. MUMFIE is a trademark of Britt Allcroft (Mumfie) Ltd.
The BRITT ALLCROFT logo is a trademark of The Britt Allcroft Group Ltd.
www.randomhouse.com/kids

Library of Congress Cataloging-in-Publication Data
Allcroft, Britt.   Britt Allcroft's magic adventures of Mumfie / created by Britt Allcroft
from the works of Katharine Tozer ; illustrations by Ken Edwards.   p.   cm.
SUMMARY: Mumfie the elephant saves his friends Whale, Pinkey the pig, and Scarecrow from
the evil Secretary, who is trying to steal the magic powers of the Queen of Night.
ISBN 0-375-80097-2
[1. Fantasy.]
I. Title: Magic adventures of Mumfie. II. Tozer, Katharine, 1907–1943. III. Edwards, Ken, 1965– ill.
IV. Title.   PZ7.A4143 Br   [E]—dc21   00-023871

Printed in the United States of America   January 2001   10 9 8 7 6 5 4 3 2 1
RANDOM HOUSE and colophon are registered trademarks of Random House, Inc.

Britt Allcroft's Magic Adventures of MUMFIE™

created by Britt Allcroft from the works of Katharine Tozer

illustrations by Ken Edwards

Random House New York

MUMFIE is a special little elephant who used to live alone in the woods. One morning, he decided to have an adventure.

Mumfie was walking through a field, humming, when suddenly he saw a man! The man was made of straw and looked very sad. "What's wrong?" Mumfie asked.

"My farm was sold and I was left behind," said the straw man.

"Why don't you come with me?" said the little elephant. "My name is Mumfie and I'm going on an adventure."

"My name is Scarecrow," said the straw man. "And I'll come with you because I don't want to be lonely."

Mumfie and Scarecrow walked for a long time. They were passing a haystack when they heard a strange noise. It was coming from inside the hay! The two friends stopped to investigate. The source of the noise was a little winged...pig! "Shhh! I'm hiding," said the pig. "The other pigs laugh at me. I want to go home."

"Where is your home?" Mumfie asked.

"On a beautiful island in the big blue sea," said the pig. "My name is Pinkey, and my mother brought me here to keep me safe. I haven't seen her since." Pinkey began to cry softly. "I want to find her."

"Then we'll help you find her," said Mumfie.

The three walked until they arrived at the sea. They saw a
whale stranded on the beach. Mumfie, Scarecrow, and Pinkey
helped the whale—who called himself Whale—back into the
water. Whale was so grateful that he offered to help the friends
find Pinkey's mother.

The trio climbed onto Whale's back and set out to sea.

"There it is!" cried Pinkey. She pointed to a tiny island in the distance.

Something about the place worried Whale. "I sense danger on that island," he said.

"But we must find Pinkey's mother!" said Mumfie.

"Very true," said Whale, and he swam onward.

The island was strangely silent. Mumfie, Scarecrow, and Pinkey stood at the shore and said good-bye to Whale. Then they headed into the dark, silent woods. Everywhere they went they saw signs hanging from the trees.

"Listen to this," said Scarecrow. He read three of the signs: "No Whistling. No Dancing. No Singing."

"No singing? Well. . . we'll see about that!" said Mumfie. He began to hum a tune.

Suddenly, from out of nowhere, a black cat
appeared! "You shouldn't have done that!" said the cat.
"Now you're in trouble!" Then Mumfie and the cat
simply vanished.

Mumfie found himself in a room filled from floor to ceiling with bottles. The bottles were labeled with the names of different sounds: PEOPLE SINGING, BEES BUZZING, WIND CHIMES TINKLING, CHILDREN LAUGHING, and so on. Mumfie was confused.

"This used to be a happy place before he took over," said a voice from behind the bottles.

"Who's there?" asked Mumfie.

A large gray bird appeared. "My name is Napoleon," he said.
"The Queen of Night used to rule this island. Then the evil
Secretary stole her magic and bottled up all the beautiful sounds."

"That's terrible," said Mumfie. "I would like to help you if I can."

Napoleon handed Mumfie a pink heart-shaped gem. "This is the
Queen's magic jewel," he said. "If the Secretary finds it, the island is
doomed. Please protect it. You are our only hope."

A long, dark shadow fell across the floor. The Secretary was
coming! With him was the black cat. Mumfie and Napoleon hid.

"When I find the Queen's jewel, my power will be complete,"
the Secretary cackled.

Napoleon whispered in Mumfie's ear. "Now you know why the
jewel must be kept from him."

Back in the woods, Scarecrow and Pinkey were very worried indeed. What had happened to Mumfie? Then they had an idea. They started to sing and—just like Mumfie—they too disappeared. But they found themselves in a different room, with a small glowing ball of light. The light began to grow bigger and took the shape of a beautiful woman. "I am Her Majesty, the Queen of Night," said the woman. "I am in search of the Secretary."

"I'm Scarecrow, and this is Pinkey," said the straw man. The little pig huddled at his feet. "I'm afraid we don't know any Secretary. Why do you want to find him?"

"The Secretary has stolen my Cloak of Dreams," said the Queen. "He plans to use its powers to turn all good into evil. I must find the cloak and save everyone on the island. The cloak is large enough to cover the world, yet small enough to fit in a thimble. Please help me!" And with that, the Queen vanished in a sparkling cloud of dust.

While Mumfie and Napoleon searched for a place to hide the magic jewel, Scarecrow and Pinkey looked for the Queen's cloak. But instead of finding either thing, they all found each other! The friends quickly exchanged stories.

"We must find the cloak at once and return it and the jewel to the Queen!" said Mumfie. But before the friends could go looking, the Secretary appeared. He locked Mumfie, Napoleon, and Pinkey in a cell.

Only Scarecrow escaped.

Scarecrow was able to return to his friends and set them free.
But as they ran from the Secretary's guards, they became trapped
in a tower room. It had only one window.

While Mumfie, Pinkey, and Napoleon held the door shut, Scarecrow grabbed a crystal from the floor and used it to smash the window. The glass shattered, as did the crystal. Among the sparkling pieces in Scarecrow's hand, he found a small thimble. Colors swirled inside it.

The Queen had said the Cloak of Dreams was small enough
to fit in a thimble! "This is the Queen of Night's magic cloak!"
Scarecrow cried. "We must give this to her right away!" Then he
and Mumfie climbed on Napoleon's back and followed Pinkey
out the window.

When they found the Queen in her garden, Mumfie
presented her with the thimble. Unbeknownst to them, the
Secretary was hiding nearby. The cloak rose from the thimble in
a mist of swirling color and instantly wrapped itself around the
Secretary. His powers were immediately destroyed.

"Now it is time to free my subjects," said the Queen. She waved her hand and the cloak rose into the sky. As it flew around the island, its magic powers freed all the islanders, including Pinkey's mother. The two pigs were finally reunited.

"Your Majesty," Mumfie said with a bow, "I have here your jewel."

"You may keep it," said the Queen, smiling. "It will keep you safe on your next adventure—and that is to go home."

Scarecrow and Mumfie found Whale waiting for them at the beach. He'd been worried about them and had come to see if he could help. The little elephant and the straw man gladly climbed onto his back and he sailed away.

When Mumfie arrived back at his house in the woods, he could hear birds singing and bees buzzing. He smiled his biggest smile. It had been quite an adventure. And home had never seemed so sweet.